For Mum and Dad, and all the books
you read to me ~ S J

Para todos los tejones que
saben ver el mundo de colores ~ C S

LITTLE TIGER PRESS LTD,
an imprint of the Little Tiger Group
1 Coda Studios,
189 Munster Road,
London SW6 6AW
www.littletiger.co.uk

First published in Great Britain 2018

Text written by Stella J Jones
Text copyright © Little Tiger Press 2018
Illustrations copyright © Carmen Saldaña / Good Illustration Ltd 2018
Carmen Saldaña has asserted her right to be identified as the illustrator
of this work under the Copyright, Designs and Patents Act, 1988
A CIP catalogue record for this book is available from the British Library

THE ONLY WAY IS BADGER

Stella J Jones   Carmen Saldaña

LITTLE TIGER

LONDON

THE ONLY
WAY IS
BADGER!

BADGERS
ARE
BEST!

Deep in the forest something wasn't right.
Overnight, a wall had appeared.
And someone had covered the trees with
strange posters.

"**Badgers** are best?" pondered Beaver.
"Be more **Badger**?" puzzled Bear.
"Whatever does it mean?"

Everyone was confused. But not for long . . .

"I'm only telling it like it is,"
said Badger.
"**Everyone** knows that
badgers are best."

"Really?"
whispered the other animals.

"He sounds so sure," muttered Moose.
"He must be right."

"Of course I'm right!"
beamed Badger.
"And, as of today, I think you all
need to make an effort to be a
bit more **badger**."

"Hang on a minute!" spluttered Deer.

"I'm only trying to help you out!" Badger butted in.

"Look, I've made a list. Number one – can you dig like a badger? Ready . . .

dig,

dig,

dig!"

"It's no good," said Deer. "These hooves weren't made for digging."

"Evidently not," agreed Badger.
"I'm afraid you'll have to leave."
"Leave?" asked Deer.

Badger nodded.

"No deer here!" he chanted.

"No deer here!

No deer here!"

"I really think—"
started Moose.
"I agree!"
Badger interrupted.
"The wood's starting
to feel more
badgery already!

Now, item two . . ."

"... badgers live in burrows, so if you can fit through this door then you can stay."

"Easy-peasy!" said the smaller woodland creatures as they skipped through the hole.

Ooh, I hope there's tea and cake!

But some got stuck.

"It's no use," mumbled Moose.
"My bum's too big!" bellowed Bear.

"Sorry guys," said Badger.
"You just don't **fit**.
So bye-bye, Bear.
Move along, Moose!"

Badger beamed at the remaining animals.
"You guys are doing great!" he cheered.

"Now it's time for your best badger bark!
So take a deep breath, and with me . . ."

Badger shook his head.
  "That was **TERRIBLE!**
You sound nothing like badgers.
I'm afraid it's time for you to hop off,
Hedgehog. Bunny, you're banned.
And Beaver, you're a leaver.

The rest of you, you're in!"

Badger admired the
black and white signs.
His shiny black and
white door. And Raccoon
and Skunk – both perfectly
black and white.
"Ahhh. Fantastic!" he sighed.

"You're too colourful!"
Badger tutted.
"Scoot, skedaddle and
vamoose!"
And he shooed them
all over the wall.

And then he spotted
the birds, the bugs
and the butterflies.

Hi guys!

You're welcome over here!

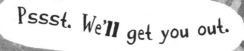

"Hey!" cried Raccoon and Skunk.
"That's so—"

   "So much better!" butted in Badger.
"This place is badgery brilliant!"

Raccoon and Skunk weren't so sure.

It's much nicer over here.

"Grab a paintbrush, buddies,"
called Badger.
"Let's get painting!
If it's not black and white
then it's just not right!"

Badger beavered away all day.
"Isn't this perfection?" he smiled.
But no one replied, because there
was no one left but Badger.

The only way is badger!

Badgers are best!

On the other side of the wall there was
colour, and fun, and laughter.
Badger stopped. He was all alone.

"Oh dear," he sniffed sadly.
And he painted one last sign.

I'M SORRY!

At last he understood.
Badgers aren't best.

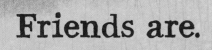

Friends are.